heat and hard candies

SURVIVAL OF THE MATED

LOLA GLASS

Cover by Francesca Michelon
https://www.merrybookround.com/

*To all of hummus and pita chips sacrificed in the making of
this book
I also wish you were chocolate*

LAUNA

I HIT the button to replay the last episode of the fourth season of *Survival of the Mated* for at least the hundredth time. Boxes containing everything I owned were stacked neatly in the kitchen, but I was focused on the show.

Did I have it memorized?

Yes.

Was I going to watch it again anyway?

Also yes.

It wasn't a comfort thing. I didn't feel a shred of happiness in watching the reality game show that centered around fae men competing to vote each other off for a chance to win a compatible mate at the end of the game.

No, it didn't make me happy.

But it did prepare me.

Because I was going to be the compatible mate in Survival's sixth season.

And unlike all of the other women who had played, I had *asked* to be put on Survival instead of Bachelorette.

Repeatedly.

Until they finally gave in and swapped me out for the sixth season's planned compatible lady.

I'd seen every episode of the show, again and again. I knew most of the men who were playing, thanks to watching.

And I knew which one I wanted to spend my life with, since marriage and mating were required at the end of the game.

The guys who played on Bachelorette were basically a different breed from the Survival guys, and I didn't want them.

So, I was willingly walking into Survival of the Mated.

Stupid decision?

Probably.

But it was better than the alternative, and I was confident my plan would work.

Mostly confident.

Fairly confident.

Confident*ish*.

As long as the guy I wanted hadn't quit or gotten mated during the fifth season, which I hadn't seen yet. It would've just finished filming. And though the Society gave out early copies of the episodes to the women who would be playing soon, they didn't give them out *that* early.

So, there was some amount of going in blind.

I hoped it would work out anyway. I didn't really have a backup plan, but I knew which of the guys were the kind I'd be comfortable mating with.

I was prepared, though.

I was going to get to the end of the show with the fae male I wanted to mate with, end of discussion.

"It's time, Launa," my fae guard said.

He was big and burly, with tan skin and curly hair tied up in a man bun. His name was Alfredo, and though he was pretty, he was about as interesting as a box of dried pasta. I had no idea what kind of fae he was, or what magic he possessed, but I didn't care.

Unlike the guard for Molly, who was in *Survival*'s first season, Alfredo definitely wouldn't be competing for me. Even if he did, I'd never choose him. All he ever talked about was the gym. It drove me damn near insane. Thankfully, I had books to occupy my time.

So many glorious books.

"Give me two more minutes," I said, wanting to watch the conversation that was playing out between two men on the screen.

I knew how it would go, but I didn't want to miss something.

Not when my future was on the line.

Being a compatible mate made living as a human pretty difficult, but getting stuck with whichever guy made it to the end, without having input?

Infinitely shittier.

Alfredo sighed, but didn't argue.

He'd been tired of me since the first hour we met.

I didn't really blame him. I could be a lot to handle. I wasn't the kind of girl who did *anything* without finding out why and establishing whether or not it mattered to me.

Which is why I knew which guy I wanted and needed.

Kyle was going to be mine. He just didn't know it yet.

two

KYLE

"LAST SEASON BEFORE BREAK," Kaden whooped, slapping me on the shoulder. A few of the other guys hollered with him, bumping elbows and slapping each other on the back.

"I need to double my weight in our month off," Jim grumbled. "I'm a fucking stick."

"So is Kyle." Ed, the new guy, bumped his elbow against mine.

Because he was a new contestant, he knew I'd helped some of the other guys win. He'd pulled me aside earlier to tell me it had been a good move, and that he agreed with me.

The women had wanted them, not me.

And I wasn't particularly confident that it was even possible for a human woman to like me at that point.

Which didn't exactly make me excited for the final season.

Of course, *Survival* would go on after all of the men took a month off to recover. There were too many unmated bastards left to end the game. And enough compatible mates to go around, as we were discovering.

But for me, season six would be my last.

I only had two or three months left in me. After I helped one last bastard mate with his perfect female, I was going to spend the final days of my life with my family. I'd be home in time to help set up for the wedding, and watch my little sister get married. After they went off on their honeymoon, I'd play board games with my parents and a few close friends until my final hours passed.

It would be a good way to go out.

"He'll still beat us in every damn physical challenge," Jim complained. "It's not fucking fair."

"You just need to try harder," Nate said, slapping him on the leg. He'd been last season's new guy, and was too nice for *Survival*.

Then again, maybe I'd become too nice for *Survival* too, considering I'd spent the past four months starving while fighting for other bastards to be with their mates.

I'd been holding out hope that a human female who might like me would appear, but hadn't had any luck.

"It's time," Ian called out, as he opened the door to the plane. A few of the guys shifted to their fae forms and jumped out immediately, wanting to be the first to get a look at the new girl.

"You okay?" Nate asked me, as a few more guys jumped.

"I'm good." I flashed him a grin that didn't meet my eyes.

Yeah, he was nicer than me.

Way too nice for *Survival*.

The two of us were the last to jump. Instead of looking down at the new woman from above, I let myself appreciate the view of our island. We'd had to move to another part of the world after the many storms of the second season, but it was stunning. Bright blue water, crisp white sand, and tall, leafy palm trees.

It didn't get better than that.

I landed beside Nate, and finally looked at the woman standing next to Jordan.

Damn.

I didn't particularly care what a woman looked like. I liked all of them. Skinny, curvy, round... a woman was a woman, and they were all beautiful.

But this one, even more so.

She was taller than most human females, with naturally tan skin and dark brown hair parted down the middle, then woven in two French braids. Her eyes were sharp, though I couldn't see the color from where I stood.

She was built strong, not slim, and wore a pair of tight black shorts that came to the middle of her thighs. A well-worn, oversized pink t-shirt hung over a good portion of the shorts and said, *"I like big books and I cannot lie"*.

Jordan introduced her as Launa, a human female who had just graduated with a master's degree in English.

It was kind of a useless degree, unless you knew you were going to be mated to a fae. Being mated to a fae meant there was no need to work or make money, and left the woman free to pursue her interests.

Launa wouldn't be into me. I wouldn't let myself consider that a possibility. Getting my hopes up was pointless.

Instead, I glanced down the row of men, trying to decide which of them I'd end up pairing with her. Somehow, I'd become Cupid.

I'd decided to hedge my bets on Kaden when Jordan announced the beginning of the challenge. It was a bag hunt, like the first challenge always was. Thanks to the luck of the genetic draw, my senses were better than any of the other guys', so challenges like that came easy.

Letting someone else win would ruin my chance to help hook the new girl up with Kaden. So, I had to win the way I always did.

Even if I was too exhausted to truly care.

I flew into the jungle at Jordan's signal, ready to get the challenge over with. A few of the guys followed me, hoping they'd spot the bags before I did, but they didn't. And no one bothered starting a fight over it anymore. Living on the island was rough enough without adding bleeding wounds to it.

I scooped the bag up without a problem, and grabbed a spare no one had noticed on the way back, before I broke through the tree line alongside a few other bastards.

They whooped, and I did the same, though I didn't feel a damn shred of enthusiasm.

One last month.

I could survive one last month on the island.

It wasn't even a month—the game had been reduced to twenty-six days after the storms forced us to cut the second season short.

I could handle twenty-six more days.

On top of shortening the game after that season, they'd altered the rewards for all of the challenges. Every reward was at least twelve hours away from the island, and they were one-on-one, so it was just the winner and the compatible female.

I usually won five or six of the nine challenges, so I really only had to survive twenty-one days.

That was even more manageable.

After the challenge was over, Jordan gave his shpeal about the island.

Then, I handed my bags to one of the other guys before following Jordan and Launa to the boat that would be taking us out for snorkeling and food.

I didn't let myself check the lady out again as we went.

There was still no point in getting attached. Or interested.

Even if she was hot as fuck.

I'd stuffed myself with food before we got on the plane two hours earlier, but my body was still trying to recover from five months of hell. So, I was still hungry.

After the speedboat reached the larger sailboat we'd be taking, I loaded my plate with burgers haphazardly. Launa followed behind me, eyeing everything but not taking a plate of her own.

"You need to eat while you can," I told her, grabbing a second plate and loading it up slightly more carefully than I did mine. "Even if you're not hungry, or you're seasick. You'll need the calories later."

"I'm allergic to dairy," she admitted. "And gluten. And peanuts, though that doesn't seem relevant right now."

I paused. "Why the fuck did they choose burgers, then?"

"I don't know."

"Here." I handed her both of the plates I'd made. "Sit down. These are for me. I'll fix it."

She bit her lip and nodded, her eyes bright with... something.

Something I wasn't going to let myself look into.

She was probably trying to decide how to tell me she was in love with Kaden and needed my help to woo him.

I scraped a thick layer of cheese off a hamburger patty. "How allergic are you to dairy?"

"Not deathly."

"Alright, what about ketchup?" I glanced at the bottle.

"Toss it to me, and I'll check."

I grabbed it. "What am I looking for?"

"It should list the allergens at the bottom of the label, usually. I'm actually allergic to gluten, not just intolerant, so I can't touch it."

I scanned the list. "Yeah, it's got wheat. No ketchup for you. This is going to be a sad meal," I warned, loading two newly cheese-free patties on top of some lettuce before throwing potato chips on the plate with it.

Afterward, I paused. "What about the patties?"

A glance back at her showed more hesitance.

Too much more hesitance.

"I probably shouldn't risk it. I'm sorry," she said quickly.

"Don't apologize." I scanned the food items. There was a fruit salad. A pasta salad. And a shit ton of potato chips. Looking at Jordan, I said, "Go ask the chef if they put anything on the fruit."

If anyone else had ordered him to leave, he would've been suspicious, but Jordan and I were cool. He usually helped me out when he could, given my history of working with the human women.

He dipped his head. "I'll make sure the Society handles the rest of the rewards better. I don't think her allergies made it into the paperwork."

"That's ridiculous."

"I know. I'll talk to the showrunners."

He slipped away, leaving me with Launa and a few of the boat's crew members.

I checked the labels on all of the bags of potato chips, then took the two that qualified over to the table with me. "This probably isn't that appetizing, but calories are calories," I said, plopping down in the chair across from hers as I handed the bags over.

"Thanks for doing that," she said, her cheeks red with embarrassment.

The woman was probably worried about the coming conversation, which would undoubtedly be about the guy she wanted.

If she always blushed like that, she was going to have a hard time influencing the game, which would make my job harder.

It was what it was, though.

"We can talk about who you want me to pair you off with after we eat. I'm sure that's what you're blushing about, but there's no rush." I grabbed a burger and took a bite.

Her cheeks reddened more.

She looked down at her bag of chips, though she didn't make a move to eat any of them. Some part of me was worried about how well she'd fare in the game if she didn't get enough to eat, but logically, she should've arrived to the island with a full stomach. The Society had been treating the compatible females much better in the last few seasons.

I ate slowly, trying to relish the meal. I'd be back to starving soon enough, and there were only so many meals left in my life. It'd be nice to get back to my house, to have the chance to cook for myself in my own kitchen again. Living on an island had gotten really damn old.

After confirming that the fruit was safe, Jordan brought the whole bowl to our table and apologized for the chef, who was apparently already at work cooking something differ-ent. Launa thanked him, but didn't touch the fruit.

"Are you worried about it?" I asked her, my forehead creasing.

"Hmm? About what?" she looked at me, her expression sheepish after missing what my question was about.

"The food." I gestured to the fruit.

"Oh, no. I just get nauseous when I'm nervous," she admitted.

"What are you nervous about?"

Her blush came back full-swing.

She was stupidly attractive. I tried not to notice.

"This conversation," she said.

I wasn't done eating, but if she was that nervous, the rest of the burgers could wait.

I wiped my hands on the napkins provided and leaned back in my chair. "Let's get it over with, then. Who do you want me to pair you off with? I get the vibes that you'll get along well with Kaden, or—"

"You," she blurted.

I blinked.

"I saw the other seasons," she added hastily. "The way you helped the other women. The life you offered them. Your personality. If I get to choose a mate, I want to choose you."

A moment of silence passed.

"If that's okay," she added, her face even redder. "I didn't really phrase that right. I—"

My eyes narrowed. "Don't bullshit me, Beautiful."

"You don't believe me?" She frowned, her face still bright red. "Why not?"

"I'm well aware that I annoy human women."

"Maybe some of them. But you're outgoing, and playful, and thoughtful. And gorgeous—really gorgeous. I want a guy like that. You—I want you." She let out a breath. "I'm not selling this very well. I'm shitty at social inter-action. This is why they wanted me to play *Bache-lorette*."

"What?"

She rubbed the back of her neck. "I kind of wrote a passionate letter—or ten—to convince the Society to let me play Survival. I've seen all of the episodes of all of the available seasons dozens of times. I've been studying it since the beginning."

"And you want me to believe that you want *me*?" My voice was skeptical.

Something in her expression grew steely. "Yes."

I didn't believe her.

It must've been apparent in my gaze, because she changed gears and asked, "How can I prove it?"

"Kiss me," I said.

If she had really seen all of the episodes of every season, she knew none of the other human women had even *liked* having any kind of physical contact with me. It was a bit of a confidence killer.

I'd be damn glad when the game was over.

"Kiss you?" The shock in her voice told me she wouldn't do it.

"Mmhm."

The redness on her face spread down her neck and over her collarbone. I'd never seen a woman blush like that, and somehow, it just made her more appealing.

I needed to stop thinking that way. She would belong to someone else.

She stood slowly.

Then walked around the table.

When I made no move to get up, she stiffly sat down on my lap. My cock hardened immediately—hell, it was already hard at the possibility that a compatible mate might be somewhat interested in me—but I didn't acknowledge it.

"I've never kissed anyone before," she said, then pressed her lips to mine.

The words registered with the hard, tense contact of our mouths.

She *what*?

If the woman had never kissed anyone, it was my responsibility to make it good for her.

Lifting a hand to her chin, I tilted her head slightly and parted her lips with my tongue. She opened for me without hesitation, and made a noise of pleasure as the kiss deepened.

My free hand caught her waist, adjusting her position to make her more comfortable. She moved her hips slightly, until my erection was pressed against her center.

She was uncertain at first, but her hands found my hair as she started kissing me back. And *fuck*, there were fireworks.

Launa kissed me like I was the air she needed to breathe.

Like she was starving, and I was food.

Like—

Like she legitimately wanted me to be her mate.

Holy fuck.

She wasn't bullshitting me.

I ripped my mouth away from hers. Our chests rose and fell heavily together, and the red of her blush had spread down into her pink shirt.

I wanted to strip it off her body and drag my tongue over every inch of her.

"You want me?" I demanded.

She nodded. "Get us to the end, and I'm yours."

I grabbed her face, capturing her mouth again.

Her fingers tightened in my hair, pulling the strands and driving me mad. I pulled her against me harder as I made love to her mouth, and she rocked her hips.

When I couldn't take it anymore, my fingers hooked in the bottom hem of her shirt.

"What do you say we make this a first kiss for the books?" I asked, my chest rumbling.

Her eyes were dilated when they met mine. *"Please."*

My cock throbbed against her, and she rocked again. "You want me to stop, you say the word."

"I know. I won't."

I tugged her shirt over her head and dropped it on the floor beside us.

Beneath it, she had on a light pink bikini top with flowers embroidered on it. It showed her tits off perfectly.

I dragged my hands up the slight curve of her waist, giving her time to tell me not to touch her. But when my hands reached the sexy swell of her breasts, she just watched me squeeze them.

"You're growling," she whispered.

"Am I?" The word came out gravelly.

She laughed softly.

I rumbled as her tits bounced lightly in my hands. "I need these bare."

"Do you think there's a closet or something on this boat?" Her cheeks were flushed. "I don't love the cameras."

My cock throbbed again. "Don't tempt me, Beautiful."

"You promised me a first kiss to remember."

"I did, didn't I?"

She nodded.

I wasn't about to turn the woman down. Not when I was living a fucking wet dream that might actually be the key to surviving.

So I let go of her breasts and stood, lifting her with me. Launa laughed breathlessly as I carried her into the main part of the boat backward.

Jordan pointed to a door, and I nodded in thanks before carrying her inside.

three

LAUNA

A DREAM.

I was living an absolute dream.

I'd totally screwed up my explanation to Kyle about why I wanted to mate with him, but by some miracle, he didn't hate me.

He called me beautiful.

He *wanted* me.

And he *kissed* me.

I'd read hundreds of steamy books, hoping I'd eventually have some kind of hot moment of my own, and there I was.

Making out with an insanely gorgeous fae on a boat, in the middle of the ocean.

Watching him touch my breasts like he wanted to worship them.

Feeling his erection against my center.

It was *incredible*.

And I needed more. So much more.

The door shut behind us, and he locked it.

I didn't turn my head to check out our closet.

I didn't care about the closet.

I just wanted him to keep touching me.

Hell, I just *needed* him to keep touching me.

Kyle took a few more steps, and I frowned when my back didn't meet a wall.

Instead, he sat down on the edge of a mattress.

Ohhh.

I'd asked for a closet, and he'd found us a room.

Perfect.

He was perfect.

His hands returned to my breasts, and I sucked in a breath at the sensation. He dragged his thumbs over my nipples, and it felt electric despite the fabric between us.

"Where were we, Beautiful?" he murmured the words, and I arched a little against his erection, trying to put him where I needed him.

"You were going to take my top off," I breathed.

"We could have fun with it on, if you'd rather." He teased my nipples again.

"No, take it off."

Reaching behind me, he found the bow. His mouth met mine again, and he made love to my tongue as he slowly untied the double knot holding it in place.

When it came undone, he let go of my mouth and leaned back just far enough to pull the fabric over my head.

Worry tensed in my abdomen for a moment, but the desire in his eyes was so thick, it faded immediately.

"The world's most perfect breasts," he said, taking them in his hands.

I couldn't stop the gasp that escaped me with his touch.

He rumbled. "You like the way it feels when I touch you here?"

"So much." The words were nearly a moan. "Don't stop."

"What if I can make it even better?"

"*Please.*"

He chuckled, and released my breasts. Before I could miss the contact, he rolled me to my back and positioned himself over the top of me.

My entire body flooded with heat.

I wanted him to rock against me, to show me how much he wanted me, but he leaned on his side instead.

When his fingers hooked in the waistband of my shorts, I couldn't look away.

"These need to go," he said, watching my face.

"They do," I breathed.

His lips curved wickedly, and I lifted my hips as he pulled them down my thighs, just a few inches. "Damn, you're soaked for me."

"Kyle." My voice was a plea.

"Don't beg me, Beautiful. Tell me. I'm yours."

My entire body shivered at the intensity in his voice. "Touch me."

His smile widened. "Here?" He dragged his fingers lightly up the inside of my thigh, inches from where I wanted him. He hadn't pulled my shorts and bottoms down all of the way, so my legs were trapped a bit, but it made the moment feel more intense somehow.

I grabbed his hand, lifted it to my core, and set his fingers where I wanted them. Then, I grabbed his arm. I wasn't sure whether I was holding it in place, or holding on to it like an anchor.

His eyes grew molten, and he slowly dragged a finger through the slickness of my folds. The satisfaction in his eyes when my hips jerked told me he knew he'd done it right.

I loved that.

The confidence.

The pride.

It was the sexiest thing on the planet. And something I could use a lot more of in my life.

"I'm supposed to be kissing you," he murmured, lowering his lips to one of my breasts. When he sucked my nipple between his lips, I cried out in pleasure.

My hips jerked as he stroked my clit slowly.

We'd only just started, but I was close to the edge. Ridiculously close.

He kept touching me and kissing me, and I just couldn't take it.

I gripped his arm desperately as I cried out with pleasure, my hips rocking through my orgasm.

The way Kyle kept stroking me told me he wasn't done.

"Have you ever climaxed for someone, Beautiful?" he asked me, his lips barely above my breast.

I shook my head, breathing too quickly to speak.

"Good. This perfect little body was made for me, and no one else." He sucked my nipple again, harder.

"I want you to fuck me," I panted. "Before we go to the island. I don't know why. I just—"

"You don't need a reason to want me." He tapped my clit lightly, and I gasped again. "I'm yours, remember?"

I nodded.

"But if I have you," he said, eyes gleaming, "I'm not going to settle for having you once. You'll have to be okay with coming back to this room every time I want you while we're on this boat."

"Alright. But you have to come back here when I want you, too."

The words earned me another wicked grin that made my toes curl. "That's my girl."

He sucked on my nipple one last time, then took the other one between his lips and worked it hard. My hips rocked as he played with them, his fingers still teasing my clit and making me hotter.

"You said you were going to fuck me," I managed, as he brought me closer to the edge.

"After I've made this the best first kiss possible, I will."

"That already happened."

He chuckled, his chest vibrating against my abdomen. "Beautiful, I haven't even kissed your clit yet."

I sucked in a breath.

He kissed his way down my abdomen, and finally tugged my shorts the rest of the way off as his knees hit the ground. His hot gaze was on my center as I struggled to keep breathing, my climax so close I could almost taste it.

"I don't want you losing it until my tongue's inside you, Launa." He lifted his gaze to mine. "Understand?"

"Why?"

"I want to taste your pleasure."

He dragged his tongue slowly over my clit.

My entire body arched off the bed, and I cried out loudly.

Kyle pulled away before my pleasure peaked, and my eyes stung at the sharp intensity.

"Put your tongue in me, now," I commanded, though it came out more like another plea.

He didn't call me on it—instead, he slid his thick tongue inside me.

The tip of it hit some sensitive part inside me, and his thumb teased my clit.

I detonated like a bomb.

My cries filled the air, my hips jerking violently.

Kyle growled against me, vibrating roughly as my pleasure coated his tongue. He licked me clean as I came down from the high, and dragged the stubble of his chin down my inner thigh as he released my core.

"You're so fucking delicious." His voice was still low, and rumbly.

"Where are you going?" I asked, noticing he'd started retreating.

"Giving you time to recover. We'll come back for more after I feed you." He dragged his whole hand over my slick core, as if he couldn't help himself.

"No." I lifted myself up on my forearms, though I was still recovering from that last orgasm. "Take your pants off."

His eyes narrowed at me. "I haven't stretched you with my fingers. Or—"

"I don't care, Kyle."

"You're a virgin, Beautiful. At least—"

"You said you were mine."

He rumbled again. "I am."

"Prove it."

He growled, but a heartbeat later, he was stripping out of his pants. The Survival episodes had blurred his cock when he was walking around naked in the first season, so I hadn't seen it before, but damn.

Hot freaking damn.

I'd seen some pretty intense fanart before, but nothing prepared me for the thick, heavy cock on the man I'd chosen.

Maybe he had a point about the stretching thing.

But, I wasn't going back now. Not that I even wanted to. Vaginas were meant to stretch.

He stepped up to me, and I sat up, reaching for his length. He rumbled when I wrapped my fingers around him, and it was a completely different kind of rumble than the last one.

He wasn't angry.

He was turned on.

"I'm supposed to be able to fit this in my mouth," I said, leaning forward to wrap my lips around the tip of him.

He throbbed hard against my mouth, and my lips stretched in a smile.

"Beautiful," he warned, as I sucked lightly. "You'll be choking on my pleasure in about three seconds if you keep that up. I've spent a long-ass time on this island, and masturbating is damn near impossible."

I released his cock long enough to look up at him. "You haven't had an orgasm in five months?"

"Give or take a few days."

"I want to choke on your pleasure, then."

He swore viciously as I took him in my mouth again, sucking lightly. When I dragged my tongue up against the underside of him, he snarled, buried his fingers in my hair, and lost it.

The taste of him flooded my senses, and I swallowed his release without choking at all.

My thighs were absolutely soaked with my desire, though.

Kyle pulled himself from my mouth a moment before he rolled us onto the bed, setting me on top of him. His cock was between my thighs, still throbbing with the aftershocks of his climax.

"You can be on top," I said, trying to catch my breath.

"Not for your first time. You control how far you take me, and stop the moment you need to," he growled back.

I lifted my hips, and he lined his tip up against my channel.

"Are you on birth control?" he asked.

"No. If it could take us a century to get pregnant, I'm not preventing it. Not ever. I want a kid eventually," I whispered.

His eyes heated more. "You're perfect for me."

"I know. I picked you, remember?" I lowered myself over him, my eyes widening at the intense stretch of him pushing into me. "You're huge."

His fingers tightened on my ass. "I don't want you in pain. Let me—" His savage groan interrupted him, as I pushed myself down further, taking him halfway inside me. The tip of him hit what I thought had to be my hymen, and it ached a little. "You're tight, Beautiful. So tight. Just let me—"

I sank down over him again, harder.

He snarled another curse. "*Launa.*"

It was painful for a moment—blindingly painful—but the moment ended quickly.

And when it was over, it was replaced with pleasure.

Insane pleasure.

I didn't have words to describe the way he felt inside me. Huge. Hard. Thick. Perfect.

None of them were accurate.

"How do you feel?" His words were a demand more than a question.

"Hot," I managed, rocking my hips just a little.

The motion was so much.

Too much.

The pleasure hit me hard—harder than I ever expected—and I screamed as I came.

Kyle roared with me, moving his hips until he hit the back of my channel. The heat of his release flooded me, melding with my own.

Our eyes were locked as we came down from the high together.

His fingers were still buried in my ass, but I didn't care. Not even a little.

"I'm never letting you go," he said.

I think it was supposed to be a warning, but it made me smile. "Neither am I."

four

LAUNA

WE GOT out of bed and reluctantly put our clothes back on. I left my shorts in the room, and Kyle didn't bother with his either, just pulling on his boxer-briefs.

Our fingers were intertwined as we walked back to the food, and found Jordan sitting at the table, staring out at the ocean.

My face had to be bright red, but I didn't say a thing as I took my seat.

Kyle didn't seem embarrassed in the slightest. In fact, the man was downright cheerful. He whistled as he filled a plate with food for me (one of the chef's staff was there to assure him it was safe).

I watched curiously.

"Be careful with him," Jordan murmured to me, and my attention jerked to my guard.

My stomach clenched.

Was he going to tell me something I didn't know about Kyle? Or—

"He's only got another month or two to live without a mate. If you're not serious about this, don't get his hopes up. He deserves to go out in peace."

My face flushed further. "I *am* serious."

Why didn't either of the men seem to believe me?

I thanked Kyle when he sat back down with a plate loaded with food I could eat, along with his burgers, which looked like they'd been warmed up.

We ate in silence, and my embarrassment faded as he asked me questions while I did.

Questions about the kinds of books I liked to read.

Fiction.

Some scientific nonfiction.

The occasional self-help book that usually offered less than a shred of useful content.

Questions about my parents.

Alive, but uninterested in maintaining a relationship with me since they learned I was going to end up mated to a fae.

Questions about my favorite foods, colors, and places.

Raspberry Sherbert (but not the sugar free kind).

Pink, because it made me feel girly and I liked that for some reason.

Beaches, though the mountains were a close second.

He asked about my degree, too.

That launched into a whole conversation about my studies on the way fictional stories affected the human brain, and the dissertation I'd started. I hoped to get my PhD at some point, though I wasn't in any hurry.

I just liked school. Learning made me feel good.

By the time the plates were empty, I felt like he knew at least as much about my life as I knew about his from watching Survival.

We arrived at the snorkeling spot shortly after that, and slipped into the water together. We stayed close as we swam around. Kyle teased my ankles and feet with the water a few times, tapping into his magic, and making us laugh. Every time I laughed, he had this proud grin on his face that made me happy.

Ridiculously happy.

When we were done swimming, there was more food ready, so we stuffed our faces some more.

When we were both full, Kyle scooped me up off the chair and carried me into the room we'd taken earlier. He shut the door before the cameras could follow us inside, and we traded mischievous smiles.

My smile didn't slip until he set me on the edge of the bed and pulled my swimsuit bottoms down.

And kissed me again.

We stayed in the room until the boat neared the Survival shore, and then Kyle finally brushed my hair away from my sweaty forehead and met my gaze. I was laying in his arms, as we both recovered from our last orgasms.

"We have to play the game to get to the end, Beautiful."

My happiness faded. "I know."

"It's only twenty-five more days. It'll be simple. You know what you need to do?"

I nodded. "I have to pretend you annoy me, like all the other women."

He agreed.

"I don't want you to worry that I'm really feeling that way."

His lips curved upward. "If you play your role right, neither of us will have to worry about that."

I lifted an eyebrow at him.

He took a strand of my hair and wrapped it around his fingers. "You should lean in to the studious image you created. Blush a lot. Act like you're uncomfortable around all the guys."

"I *am* uncomfortable around all the guys."

"Even better." He winked at me, and I rolled my eyes, though I couldn't stop myself from smiling. "There'll be so much awkward tension between you and the other guys that I won't be able to worry. They'll think you dislike me as much as the last women did, so you won't have to worry about me. It'll be easy."

Theoretically, it sounded good.

It was the same plan I'd come up with before going to the island, actually.

It just felt daunting now that it was hanging over my head.

"We've got this, Beautiful." He tugged lightly on my hair, and his confidence eased my worry just a little.

KYLE CLEANED us both up with his magic before we joined Jordan on the speedboat that would take us to shore. We positioned ourselves on opposite sides of him, and when Kyle winked at me, I rolled my eyes.

It didn't take much thinking about all the sex we'd had to make my face hot, so I focused on that for a minute. I wanted to be red and splotchy, so everyone would think I was frustrated. I definitely got red when I was frustrated. And embarrassed. And horny. And probably happy, too.

The boat landed on the shore, and Kyle immediately jumped out and offered me a hand with a grin.

We both knew I couldn't reply the way I wanted to, so instead, I huffed loudly and climbed down from the boat on my own. When I tripped at the bottom—that one was an accident—Kyle lifted me back to my feet quickly.

I grumbled at him and stepped away with a grudging, "Thanks."

He chuckled, and followed me up the beach.

A few guys had jogged over, and saw our interactions just like we'd expected.

Two of them gave Kyle bro-hugs of condolences.

Two more exchanged a look that said they wanted to work with Kyle again, for the same reason everyone wanted to work with Kyle.

They thought he was unlikable.

They thought he wasn't a threat.

And we were going to play them like a fiddle.

I ACTED AWKWARD every time one of the men tried to start a conversation with me. It didn't take a whole lot of effort, considering I legitimately felt uncomfortable every time one of them came up to me.

I could tell the guys were talking about me on and off, which added to the discomfort.

The discomfort was needed, though. I leaned on it.

It was insanely hot out, so I was dripping sweat, and kept

going to take dips in the ocean. That was a good way to get away from the men.

The water helped with the heat a little, but not enough. I kind of wished it would rain, like it had in the second season of the show.

Then again, I'd probably take sweating over shivering. I wouldn't be able to snuggle with Kyle constantly without making the other guys suspicious, so I'd have to get cozy with some of the other dudes. Yikes.

Kyle spent the day hanging out with the guys, like he always did during the other seasons. He was friends with all of them, even the complete jerks, like Jim.

Because the other guys didn't think he was a threat to win the game, it solidified the existing bonds. Everyone wanted to work with Kyle.

Including me.

I had to wonder how it would feel to be liked that much. To be that good at socializing. To enjoy being around other people to that extent.

I wanted to ask him, but that obviously wasn't going to happen.

Anyway, the day passed by slowly. I spent the night curled up in my own shelter, away from the men. The show had started treating the compatible females much better after the first two seasons, so I had a heap of blankets, a couple of pillows, and a small tarp that had been spread over my sleeping space. It wasn't a bed, but it was far more comfortable than it could've been.

The next day passed the same way the first had. At the council that night, most of the votes were against Kaden.

I remembered the way Kyle had told me he thought I would get along with Kaden, and had to bite back a smile when I realized that was why he'd been voted out.

Our eyes met over the fire for the briefest of moments as Kaden walked away, and Kyle winked at me.

He was so damn good at *Survival*.

five

LAUNA

KEEPING to myself on the island was pretty easy. I spent my days avoiding the fae guys, sitting on the beach or in the ocean, and daydreaming.

Mentally, I replayed books I had read. When I got tired of that, I mentally ran through my research, trying to come up with new angles or things I hadn't considered before. I figured out a few different things to look at, and said them aloud so they'd be on camera in case my hunger affected my memory.

Being hungry sucked, but I adjusted after day three. It felt like weakness more than anything else. We had enough rice to eat a small portion twice a day, but it barely helped.

On day 5, we finally went to the second challenge. It was a puzzle, so as soon as I saw it, disappointment set in.

Kyle wasn't going to win.

He was a big, loveable bastard, but he was shit when it came to puzzles.

Sure enough, I was on a boat with Ev an hour later. It was taking us to the *Survival* spa. Technically it was the second *Survival* spa, because the first had been left behind when the show changed locations after Erin's season. But that didn't really matter.

Ev tried to start conversations, and I ended all of them with one-word answers and looking away uncomfortably. He'd given up by the time we reached the spa.

It was going to be a long twenty-four hours alone with him, but at least Jordan was there as backup.

Ev really wasn't a bad guy, so I felt kind of guilty for trying so hard not to interact with him. But there was no point in leading him or anyone else on.

So, I tried not to feel bad as the silence set in.

We both took showers before dinnertime. Part of me worried that Kyle would get booted while I was gone, but logically, I knew that wasn't going to happen.

No one saw him as a threat to win, and everyone wanted to get to the end with him.

The spa provided robes and clean underwear, so I put mine on and tied my robe firmly in place. Though I would've preferred to keep my own clothes, I knew the spa would wash them for us, and I wanted them clean.

Ev tried to make conversation again while we ate all of the food (it was free of gluten, nuts, and dairy, thankfully), but I shut him down again.

After we were done with the food, we were led to another room for our massages.

I left all of my clothes on, and plopped down on the table face-first. When I heard Ev's clothes rustling, I squeezed my eyes shut.

Awkward.

It was so, so awkward.

AFTER THE MASSAGES, we were led to the bedroom we would share.

More discomfort ensued.

When Ev sprawled out on one side of the bed, I padded over to the large couch on the other side of the room and got cozy.

His huff of frustration was impossible to miss.

He grudgingly offered me the bed, saying he would take the couch, but I politely told him I was happier where I was. He grumbled a little more, but eventually, started snoring.

It took me a while to fall asleep, but I managed.

. . .

THE NEXT MORNING consisted of more awkwardness.

They gave us facials.

Head massages.

Foot treatments of some kind.

It was more pampering than I'd ever had, and I was highly uncomfortable with all of it. But, I gritted my teeth and made it through.

When we finally got on the speedboat and headed back to the island, I was so relieved I could've cried.

I wanted to feel Kyle's arms around me, like I had during our reward, but it wasn't an option.

So, I just held tightly to the handrail beside my seat and gritted my teeth.

Only twenty days left.

I would survive it.

The ride wasn't too long, and soon enough, we were back on the Survival beach. Ed, the only fire fae currently in the game, had been voted out. He was a decent guy, but I wouldn't miss him.

Kyle caught my gaze as some of the other men started walking off, and there was a bit of a question in it. He seemed like he was asking if I was okay.

I gave him a small smile and a nod before I headed back to my usual spot on the beach.

Only twenty more days.

It would be fine.

THREE MORE DAYS PASSED SLOWLY.

Another puzzle challenge, too.

And another reward with someone other than Kyle. That time, it was with Oz, the game's only air fae. I could tell Ev didn't try to win the challenge. He was smart enough not to want to go on another reward with me.

Oz seemed much more comfortable with silence than Ev, and didn't push me to talk too much. That made it a lot less awkward.

We spent a day and a half on a yacht, exploring a few different gorgeous locations. There was tons of food, snorkeling, and swimming, and our room was comfortable.

I really just wanted a good book to curl up with, but I tried to enjoy the experiences anyway. I didn't know if I'd ever do anything like that again after Survival ended.

On the way back to the island, Oz asked me about books.

I admitted I loved them, and tried to end the conversation—but then he asked if I'd read a certain fantasy romance book.

One of my *favorite* fantasy romance books.

I couldn't help but lean toward him, asking if he'd read it.

When he confirmed that he had, we had a long discussion about the pros and cons of the whole series. The conversation continued, loudly, on the speedboat back to the *Survival* island.

It caught me off guard when we arrived, because I was so excited about the chat.

My gaze caught on Kyle's as we got off the boat, and I found his eyes narrowed.

Shit.

He was usually calm and collected, no matter what.

He had to know that I wasn't *interested* in Oz—I just liked having someone to talk about books with.

But I couldn't come out and tell him that. If we went off alone, red flags would rise immediately. That wasn't even an option.

So, fear clenched my abdomen as I watched him force his usual laid-back demeanor.

He smacked Oz on the shoulder to welcome him back, then winked at me before sauntering off with the other guys.

My stomach clenched tighter.

I hadn't even checked to see which guy was gone, but I didn't give a damn. I needed to talk to Kyle... and I couldn't.

LAUNA

THE TENSION LINGERED through that day, and the day and a half that followed. Parker was gone, which didn't bother me in the slightest.

There was never a moment for us to slip away together.

Avoiding the other guys meant avoiding Kyle too.

The next challenge was a classic—mud wrestling—and I didn't even need to watch to know who was going to come out on top.

I *did* watch, though.

I watched closely.

There was something ridiculously hot about seeing Kyle fight with, and defeat, a bunch of massive, gorgeous fae.

He was the biggest, and the strongest.

The man was absolutely *covered* with mud when the challenge ended, but he grabbed my hand and lifted it high in the air as he whooped about his victory the way he always did in the past seasons.

The other guys laughed and shook their heads.

Typical Kyle, they were thinking.

They had no idea what had happened between us—and that made my toes curl into the sand a little.

Kyle's hand was on my back as he led me to the helicopter that would take us to the volcanic hot springs we were spending the rest of the day at.

That touch was typical for him, too. Typical enough that no one would think twice about it.

Despite it being normal for him, and despite the mud all over his hands, I relished the touch.

It had been a long, lonely ten days since our time together. My chest ached, and my stomach hurt.

As soon as the helicopter's door shut, he sat down on the bench seat and pulled me with him. His side pressed against mine, and his muddy hand gripped my thigh as the helicopter rose from the ground.

Jordan followed behind us, flying with his wings rather than in the copter.

The show had stopped allowing the men to carry the compatible women through the sky after the second season. I was pretty sure it was part of their effort to make the women feel more comfortable, and appreciated that. I didn't want to fly in anyone's arms except Kyle's, even though I couldn't admit it to anyone but him.

The helicopter landed twenty minutes later, and we both stood. Kyle's hands were on my hips as he led me out, lifting me before I could step down.

I loved the way he manhandled me, as ridiculous as it sounds. The big hands, the dominance, the bossiness...

I didn't think I'd ever get enough.

The hot springs were gorgeous, smooth pools of black stone surrounded by palm trees. There was thick, soft-looking sand on the beach nearby. I figured some kind of human or fae intervention had made the place as idyllic as it was, because it looked like something straight off a travel blog.

Kyle only gave me a moment to take the sight in before he had me pinned against a palm tree, and his mouth crashed into mine.

My fingers wrapped around his biceps as I kissed him back just as passionately as he kissed me. Our tongues and mouths fought, his erection hard and thick against my abdomen.

When he finally pulled away, his gaze was intense. Our chests heaved together, rising and falling quickly.

"Oz said you talked about books," he growled.

I nodded. "We talked about my favorite series on the way back from the reward. The rest of the trip was awkward."

"What series?"

"It's called *Forbidden Mates*. I couldn't believe he'd read them too. When I get talking about books, it's hard to stop."

"You'll tell me about them." The words were an order.

The fact that he was commanding me to tell him about books?

It was sexy as hell.

"Deal."

He kissed me again, with less anger behind it. His muddy hands slid into my messy, undone hair. I'd been dying to braid it back again ever since I washed it at the spa, but I didn't know how to do the French braids the stylists had given me before I started the game.

I kissed him back, sliding my arms around his neck and using the position to pull myself up a little higher.

He realized what I was doing, and lifted me off my feet.

My legs wrapped around his waist, and he pressed his cock against my center. Despite the fabric separating us, it felt amazing.

The kiss went on for ages before Kyle finally pulled away, growling, "If there weren't cameras here, I'd be fucking you against this tree right now."

My entire body was already flushed, but his words didn't cool me down any. "Is there anywhere private we can go?"

He looked backward. "A bathroom. It doesn't look big."

"Big enough, though?"

His eyes gleamed. "I like the way you think, Beautiful."

It had been too long since I heard him call me that.

Way too long.

There was a shower nearby with three wooden walls and a flimsy curtain to give you just enough privacy while you washed up. Kyle carried me there, first, and dropped his shorts so he could rinse the mud off him. My t-shirt followed, since he'd covered that too, and a glance at my shorts showed that they needed the same treatment.

I slipped out of them while he scrubbed himself clean with soap, his back to the flimsy curtain to block everyone else's sight.

His gaze was on me as I stripped, his attention hot and heavy. "Beautiful." I wasn't sure if he was using the nickname or just complimenting me. Either way, it made me blush.

I looked down at my swimsuit, and realized the muddy water had leaked through to it too.

My gaze lifted to Kyle's, and my body burned when I saw his fist wrapped around his cock.

My hands went around my back, and I tugged on the bow until it came undone.

His chest rumbled, and he stroked his cock slowly.

I pushed the bottoms down my thighs, and stepped out of them.

He growled. "Come here."

I stepped up to him, and he wrapped one arm around my ass before hauling me up off my feet.

My back hit the wooden wall, but thankfully, it remained planted where it was without shaking too much.

"Turn off the cameras," Kyle said, raising his voice.

Jordan sighed loudly.

"Get everyone out of here, too."

My guard's grumble made me bite my lip. "Kyle…"

"Yeah, Beautiful?" He dragged the tip of his cock over my clit, and whatever I'd been thinking died instantly.

"Never mind."

He teased me with the head of his erection again, and my head tipped back, my eyes closing. I could hear people leaving around us, but with him touching me like that, I didn't care.

Not even a little.

"You remembered who you belong to you on those rewards, right?" he asked, his voice low.

"Always." My whisper earned another stroke of his cock against me, and I moaned.

He lifted me a little higher. "Did anyone touch you?"

"Of course not."

He worked me again.

"Did they make you laugh, or smile?"

"No."

And again.

And again.

"I need you," I said, the words coming out as a plea.

"What did I say about asking, Beautiful?"

My body may as well have caught fire, I was so hot. "Give me your cock, Kyle."

"That's my girl." He lined himself up with my entrance, and filled me slowly.

My lips parted.

My mind spun.

It had been ten days—and he'd never taken me in that position before.

It was intense.

So, so intense.

I was insanely full. So full, I could barely breathe.

"Kyle." My chest rose and fell quickly. I didn't know why I was saying his name. I just was.

"You're so damn good to me," he growled, lifting me a little before he pulled me down harder.

I gasped as he bottomed out inside me.

"So fucking wet. Tight. Responsive." He squeezed my ass, and I moved against his cock, earning a growl. "Mine."

"I'm yours," I moaned, remembering the way he'd asked me to say it. Something about the words felt sort of... powerful.

He swore viciously, driving into me hard and dragging me over the edge with him as he did. I came with a cry, holding tightly as he fucked me against the wooden wall. It shook with the force, but I was too lost in my pleasure to care.

We were both breathing hard as he came down from the high, one of his hands buried in my hair and the other gripping my ass. "You can't say that while I'm inside you, Beautiful. Not until the game's over."

I frowned, worry clenching my abdomen.

Had I done something wrong?

"I'm sorry," I said quickly. "I—"

"No, Sweetheart. No. Don't apologize." He growled the words at me. "That's how we seal the bond. I want to hear the words on your lips—and feel them on mine. I want it badly. Both of us say the words while we're fucking—that's all it takes to become mates. But we can't until the game is over. We have to survive this first."

Oh.

Wow.

No wonder the words had felt powerful.

"That's why you like hearing them?" I asked.

"Yes." He moved his hips a little, making me suck in a breath. "And it satisfies the possessive beast inside me."

He was a dragon—I knew that from the previous seasons. Shifting took a lot from the guys, so I'd never seen him or any of the others shift.

I wanted to, though.

Almost as much as I wanted to see him wild with need again. That one was far more accessible.

"Does it hurt anything if I say the words and you don't?" I asked.

"No. Just makes it hard to keep myself under control."

"Why do you need to stay under control?"

"Because if I shift, my cock will grow, and I'm fucking huge. Even for a fae." The words were matter of fact, though there was still that sexy pride in his eyes.

"Okay." I acted like I was dropping the subject and leaned toward him, pressing my lips to his. He adjusted his grip on my ass and kissed me, parting my lips with his tongue.

He moved inside me slowly and smoothly, dragging me back to the edge as we made out.

I pulled away before I came again, lifting my lips to his ear and murmuring, "I'm yours, Kyle."

He snarled, his body shuddering, then swelling.

I screamed my pleasure as I came harder and faster than ever, his erection growing bigger as he fucked me.

One climax became two, then three, when the heat of his release flooded my channel.

"I wasn't done with you, wicked little thing." His words were gravel, his eyes bright and hot.

I arched on his cock, still panting as I tried to recover from my climaxes. "You can only get off twice."

"Until I recover." He carried me out of the shower, still impaled on his cock until we reached the nearest hot spring. He set me down on the ledge and slipped into the water, opening my legs wide before he looked up at me. "You're so fucking beautiful."

"You make me feel like I am," I admitted.

His chest rumbled, and he kissed my core until I was coming again, on his mouth.

Then he fucked me again.

When we finally settled into the hot springs, his arms were wrapped around me and I was sitting on his lap. The tension between us was gone completely, and I felt good. Really, really good.

Jordan and everyone else returned shortly after that, and when they did, they brought food. I tried not to make eye contact with any of them at first, feeling awkward as hell, but Kyle chatted with them and thanked them as if nothing had been weird at all.

So, my awkward feeling faded.

We sat on the rock ledge, letting our feet dangle into the spring while we ate.

When we were done, we sank back into the water, and Kyle asked me about my favorite series. He remembered the name of it, and when I launched into a basic explanation of the plot, he asked all the right questions to keep the conversation going. We talked about it for hours, and I enjoyed the discussion with him even more than the one I had with Oz.

Kyle was just... fun.

And funny.

He made things easy, and he made me happy.

I couldn't think of any more important trait I wanted in a man, other than the basics of honesty and loyalty and whatnot. But I knew him well enough from seeing him play Survival month after month to be confident that he had those traits too.

And every time we interacted, I was even more sure that I'd chosen right.

seven

KYLE

OZ WAS GONE when we got back from the hot springs that night, just like I'd planned. I'd warned Launa about it, and though she rolled her eyes at me, she couldn't hide her amusement at the way I was targeting anyone she might be interested in.

It fucking sucked to go back to acting like we weren't together, but the eleventh day was done.

Which meant there were only fifteen days left.

Barely more than two weeks.

The time was passing quickly, and we'd be done before we knew it.

The next two days were over soon enough, and then the next puzzle challenge arrived.

There had been an annoying amount of them already, but I

supposed I'd rather have my extra time with Launa spread out a bit more. So, it was fine.

I had to fight to keep my breathing even as I watched my female walk away with Travis. Of all the guys on the island, he was the only one I hated. Or even slightly disliked. The others were fine, but Travis?

Our many months on Survival together only proved how obnoxious the bastard was.

He didn't care who the compatible female wanted.

He didn't care if she didn't want him.

He didn't care which of the other guys were the nearest to death.

He didn't care about anyone but himself, and it irritated the hell out of me.

I trusted Jordan to keep Launa safe, but I didn't want Travis alone with her.

It took everything I had to act normal when we made it back to the island. Everyone wanted to talk to me alone, so I forced myself to strategize with each of them the way I always did. They all thought I was working with them, and even though they knew I was working with everyone else too, they were under the impression that they needed me badly enough to continue.

If history had proven anything, it was that they were right.

They needed me if they wanted to get to the end.

And I needed them just as badly, even if I couldn't let them realize it. All it would take was a few votes to remove me from the game.

That wasn't going to happen, of course.

But theoretically, it could.

Which was why I had to bullshit my way through the rest of the day, until Launa got back that night and eased my nerves.

So I put my fear in my pocket and went to work.

Twelve hours later, Jim was gone, and Launa returned safely. Travis spent an hour complaining about how she hadn't wanted to talk to him, and satisfaction relaxed me further.

Everything was going to work out.

I was damn sure of that.

eight

LAUNA

MY REWARD with Travis was awkward. He tried to force me to open up to him by badgering me repeatedly, and obviously failed.

By the time we got back to the beach, I was hoping I could come up with a way to make sure he was the next one out.

But ultimately, that would require actually interacting with some of the men, which was an easy no from me. I'd just have to wait and hope.

Two and a half more days passed slowly, before there was another challenge.

It was another puzzle challenge.

I was about ready to rip my damn hair out when I saw it. I wanted to spend the day with Kyle, not another guy.

I had noticed that most of the guys weren't really trying to win puzzle challenges after the first one, though. They weren't enjoying our rewards, so they weren't competing.

And I sure as hell wouldn't complain about *that*. The less they tried, the better.

Kyle still wasn't going to win when it came to puzzles, though.

I watched glumly as Colt destroyed the wooden-ball maze puzzle, and reluctantly left with him.

He was nicer than Travis, at least.

We went back to the spa, and it turned into a repeat of the misery that was my first reward challenge with Ev. Same awkward short conversations. Same clothed massages. Same sleeping on the couch.

I was even more exhausted when we got back to the beach than I had been before the reward.

Travis had gone home while I was away, so that cheered me up a little. Going back into the heat and sitting down on the sand wiped away the cheer pretty fast.

I was tired of surviving.

Whose idea was this damn game in the first place?

And why had I thought signing up was a good idea? I could've been living in luxury in the Bachelorette mansion, but instead, I was just sitting there while the sun attempted to cook me. Sunblock prevented the burn, but it didn't make it feel any less miserable.

Cold mist drifted over the back of my neck, and I suppressed a groan.

My eyes closed, and I realized that Kyle must've been using his magic on me.

Though I couldn't thank him, hug him, or even look at him, gratitude welled in my chest.

I'd made a good decision.

I was going to survive.

And then, I was going to be with him.

TWO DAYS LATER, there was another challenge.

It was *another* puzzle.

I was going to lose my damn mind if it happened again.

I spent the day snorkeling with Nate, though, and it was surprisingly neutral. He didn't ask me questions, or push me for answers. He was a lot like Oz, actually.

There was no talk about books, but by the time we got back that night, I felt like I could handle the last six days on the island.

Colt had gone home when we got back, which left us with a grand total of five men.

Kyle, Nate, Reid, Ev, and Ian.

Kyle was still the ringleader, of course. And I sincerely hoped it would stay that way.

There were only two challenges left, so there wasn't too much more ahead of us. The final challenge was always a puzzle, and was always a statue of the compatible woman the guys were competing for. So, that challenge wasn't Kyle's to win.

The second-to-last one would have to be the comfort item challenge. Sometimes they inserted it into the game earlier, and sometimes they waited to the end, but they always included it. It gave every one of the guys a chance to sit down with the woman they were competing with, so it was unique in that way.

Ever since they changed the way challenges worked, the winner would have an entire day to walk me through their bag of comfort items and relax at the spa with me.

I sincerely hoped that Kyle would win, and that we were still on the same page, because the end was approaching fast. What if he didn't want me anymore or something?

Shit, that was terrifying.

With worry hanging over my head, the next two and a half days passed slowly. But, I survived them, and made it to the challenge.

Jordan announced everyone's favorite competition: finding the bags of comfort items they had packed. The first person back would get the big reward. Everyone else would get five minutes to show me their bag and the asset folder with it. All of that was expected.

I sat on the edge of my seat, trying not to let my gaze meet Kyle's before the challenge started.

Jordan announced the beginning of the game, and the guys all took off into the forest. Some had their wings out, and some didn't.

My fingers were hooked on the edge of the bench, my heart beating rapidly as I waited for a sign of the first guy. It never took long for someone to come back. No more than five or ten minutes.

"Breathe, Launa," Jordan murmured, relaxing on the bench beside me. "He'll be the first back."

"He's never won this challenge before," I whispered back.

"He's never had a reason to."

The man wasn't wrong. But Kyle typically did his best to win all of the challenges, regardless of whether or not the girl he was competing for was into him.

"He wins the first challenge every season, and this is the easier version of it," Jordan said. "Have a little faith."

I nodded, breathing out slowly.

It was going to be fine.

Kyle was going to win, and I was going to get to spend a day with him at the spa instead of another awkward trip with someone else. I didn't want to consider not getting any more time with him before I chose him as my mate, so I had to believe that.

A pair of scaly wings broke through the tree line, and I was on my feet in a heartbeat. I barely managed to slap my hand over my mouth in time to silence myself before I could cheer aloud.

Kyle grinned broadly as he landed in front of me and Jordan, and it took everything I had not to throw myself into his arms.

I missed him.

I missed him badly.

My eyes started stinging when he winked at me, taking his seat on the bench.

Another guy came running out of the forest, and I forced myself to sit down before he saw me standing and wondered why.

My breathing evened out, my relief so thick I could taste it.

We'd get one last day together before the final challenge and the big decision.

I'd only need to survive one more uncomfortable reward afterward.

I could do it.

The rest of the guys returned quickly.

I sat through a few minutes with each of them as they showed me the treats they'd brought. Now that the show supplied me with blankets and tarps and everything, everyone just brought junk food. It was kind of fun.

Or it would've been, if I wasn't itching to leave with Kyle.

The guys all showed me their asset folders, which contained pictures of their homes and families, too. I didn't bother feigning interest; I didn't want any of them to think I had any kind of feelings for them. They were probably calling me names behind my back, but I didn't care.

I was there to mate with Kyle, not to make friends.

And I'd almost succeeded.

When the time was finally up, I followed Kyle and Jordan to the boat.

Kyle and I left space between us up until the guys were too far in the distance to see us, and then he pulled me onto his lap. A sputtered laugh escaped me as we went over a wave, rocking the entire boat and smashing me against his chest pretty hard.

"We'd be safer in our own seats," I said, fighting a grin.

"Nah, you're safest right here." He pulled me against him even tighter, inhaling deeply. "Damn, you smell good. I've missed you."

"I've missed you too." I tucked my forehead against his neck as we went over another wave, and he held me close. "Only a few more days."

"We've got this," he agreed. "Being apart during the final reward will be rough, but we'll make it."

"We will."

He kissed my cheek. "My parents are going to love you."

My chest warmed. "I hope so."

"You're saving my life, Beautiful. They'd love you even if you were a menace to the Society. My sister is one, and we're all still her biggest fans."

My lips curved. "Your sister is a menace?"

He chuckled. "You have no idea."

"Do you think she'll like me?"

"Of course she will." He squeezed me. "Rhett found her a mate a little while ago, so she's getting married pretty soon after the season ends. She likes everyone right now, from what I've heard."

"Not a bridezilla, then?" I asked.

"A what?"

I laughed, and explained the term.

"Nah, she's a bridezilla," he said with a grin. "But a loveable one. Most of the time."

Something told me that his definition of *most of the time* wasn't the same as everyone else's, if she was really considered a menace to Society.

But, that didn't matter.

I leaned against his chest, breathing in his scent.

We were together, and that was what mattered.

LAUNA

GOING to the spa with Kyle was nothing like going with the other men.

When I headed for the shower, he joined me. We washed up quickly, and as soon as the soap was off our skin, he towed me toward the bathtub. We both fit inside it, and ended up spending over an hour cuddled up beneath the hot water.

We traded stories about our childhoods and our families. It was really nice, even though it made my heart ache for what I'd lost when mine rejected me for being compatible with the fae.

Hearing about his gave me hope, though.

His family was immortal, and they were loving. According to him, they would accept me with open arms, and love me for who I was.

That sounded like pure bliss.

When we eventually washed up and made it out of the tub, we headed out for food. There was a massive spread set up for us, and we feasted for a few minutes before we started talking again.

"So, what do you want from our life together?" I asked, wiping the corner of my mouth with a napkin.

"What do I want?" he asked, lifting an eyebrow at me.

"Yes. Or what do you see our future looking like?"

His lips curved upward. "I see you focusing on your research. You grumbling at me when I insist on going with you to your university's library. Me working on my computer, in the chair next to yours."

I bit my lip, hope blossoming in my chest.

"I see myself dragging you out of there for food when you're so focused that you try to dodge meals. Us watching movies together at night, and getting together with the family for board games or card games once a week. Maybe twice, if you really like them."

He captured my hand with his free one. "I see us sneaking into the library's bathroom to fuck after I've watched you bite your lip like that too many times. Or after you read something that turns you on. I see us having lazy morning sex, and hot afternoon sex. All of the sex, actually."

I laughed. "*All* of the sex?"

"All of it," he agreed, grinning. "Mostly, I just see us

together, living life. Enjoying the little things. Even grocery shopping."

"You actually shop for your own groceries?" My eyebrows shot upward. "I was under the impression you're crazy rich."

"Even crazy rich people shop for their own groceries." He saw the skepticism in my gaze, and laughed. "Sometimes."

"That's more like it. You probably just run to the store now and then for one little thing."

"Alright, you caught me. That can still be fun though."

"I believe you. Is there anything else you see?" I took another bite of my food.

"I see you eventually growing a baby for us." He patted my very flat, very *not pregnant* stomach.

I snorted, smacking his hand away. "If we ever get lucky enough. Some fae couples never have kids, right?"

"The luck strikes most people eventually. It'll work for us at some point." He grabbed a chunk of pineapple I'd left on my plate. I didn't like pineapple, but it was mixed into the fruit bowl so there was no avoiding it. Kyle knew that, and knew I had no problem with him pulling things off my plate. It was just food.

"I hope so." I stole a grape off his plate. He'd saved them for me, even though I knew he liked them too. Maybe that was a sign of love, or at least attachment.

Then again, what was love if it wasn't attachment?

"What if I'm a terrible baby-incubator, and it never happens?" I asked, suddenly a little self-conscious. I had no control over my reproductive system. It could be a piece of shit for all I knew.

"Then we'll have a lot more free time to read books, play board games, and have all the sex." He took another piece of pineapple. "Life is good, even when it throws shit at us. We'll wade through the crap together, and have fun doing it."

I loved that perspective.

"I can't believe none of the other women who played Survival picked you. They're ridiculously stupid," I said.

He laughed. "I'm glad they didn't. I wouldn't be anywhere near as happy with them as I am with you."

"Liar. You just said you'll be happy no matter what."

"Assuming I have the world's most beautiful mate, who loves reading sexy books. And informing me of all the ways we could have sex if we lived in an alternate universe, yes. I'll be happy no matter what we go through."

I rolled my eyes. "The other women were beautiful too."

"In their own way, sure. None of them did it for me the way you do, though. I'd go through six months of this island hell all over again for you and that pretty little ass."

My face burned, but I couldn't hide my grin. "You're ridiculous."

"It's fun to be ridiculous." He grabbed more pineapple. "What do *you* see in our future?"

"All the things you see. Research. Working together. Reading. Fun. I might like to travel a little, after I've recovered from this *island hell*."

He grinned back at me. "I've never traveled much. Focused on work for the majority of my life. We can explore new places together."

"That sounds perfect." I took another one of his grapes. "You know you don't need to save these for me, right?"

"I know. I want to." He took my last chunk of pineapple. "You have to fuck me when you get horny from reading all those books. No getting yourself off."

"Fine." My face was definitely red, but I didn't mind it. He probably knew I was embarrassed anyway.

"Are you ready for bed yet, Beautiful?" Kyle asked.

"Yep." I stood, and he did too. When he offered me his elbow, I slipped my hand in the crook of it. "Only three more days."

"It's about fucking time."

Another laugh escaped me.

He pulled me closer. "That's got to be the best sound in the world."

"Don't be silly."

"I like being silly." He tucked me closer to his side. "I didn't show you what was in my care package."

"That's not the package I want to see of yours."

He barked out a laugh. "I'll show you every package I've got."

I smiled. "What did you bring?"

"Hard candies. An assload of them. No one ever brings that shit, but it's nice to have something to snack on during the long-ass days on the island."

"Good idea. Grandmas all over the world agree with you." I bumped his hip with mine. "Did you bring caramels?"

"I did."

"Then you're the perfect granny, aren't you?"

"Damn straight."

We exchanged grins, and continued to our room together.

The night was perfect.

WE ONLY HAD sex once before calling it a night, and stayed up late talking about everything under the sun.

Books.

Kinks we didn't really possess.

Food

Kinks we *did* sort of possess.

Parenting.

Board games.

Stars.

Places we wanted to see.

It was already the next morning when we finally fell asleep.

We slept through the massages we were supposed to receive, and didn't actually get out of bed until Jordan told us it was time to go.

"Only three days, Beautiful," Kyle murmured, kissing me lightly on the lips. "We've got this."

"We've got this," I agreed, though my stomach was still a little twisted.

What if something happened?

What if Kyle got voted out after the last challenge?

What if—

He kissed me again, slower.

Hotter.

My toes curled, but Jordan knocked again.

"The next time we're alone together, we're going to be sealing that mate bond." He kissed me again. "I love you, and I'm fucking glad you're mine."

My eyes stung. "What if something goes wrong?"

"Do you trust me?"

I nodded.

It hadn't been long, and *Survival* wasn't a great place to build trust, but I did trust him. He'd never given me a reason not to, and he always kept his word. I suppose seeing him do the same for multiple seasons helped with that.

"Then trust that I won't let anything go wrong. If it does, I'll figure out a way to come out on top despite it. I've got this. Okay?"

"Okay."

He gave me one last kiss before tucking me against his side and leading me out of the room.

I couldn't prevent my nerves, but his words had definitely eased them a little.

AFTER WE GOT BACK to the island, the final two days passed even slower than I thought they would. Ian was gone, but that didn't really matter to me.

More sweating occurred.

More feeling like I was being cooked by the sun, too.

And more discomfort.

But eventually, it *did* come to an end, and it was time for the final challenge.

As usual, the guys took their places in front of Jordan. I sat down on the bench off to his side, eyeing the puzzle set-up.

It was definitely the game's usual final puzzle.

A gigantic statue of me, divided into many, many pieces. I usually enjoyed puzzles, but that was one I had no desire to touch. The thing was intense.

Jordan rattled off the rules and reward (the reward was another twelve-hour sightseeing ride on the show's yacht), then had the men take their stations.

They all traded nods.

And then, they began.

No one moved quickly when they did. It wasn't a fast puzzle.

Most of the guys sorted pieces by which part of my body they resembled. Nate just went for it.

I'd seen people win with both strategies, so I knew it didn't particularly matter which one a guy went with. Sorting seemed less overwhelming to me, though.

I looked over all four men.

Nate.

Kyle.

Reid.

Ev.

I didn't know any of them well, or even a little, except Kyle. That was my fault, and I didn't regret it. But it did make me nervous.

What if Kyle was wrong?

What if he did get voted out?

Could I refuse to mate with anyone else? Was that even a possibility?

I didn't think so, but shit, I hoped it was.

Ev was the best puzzle guy in the group, but he was moving so slowly that I was pretty sure he'd ruled out any desire to mate with me.

That was good. Less competition for Kyle.

Nate was making the most progress, by a long shot. Reid was probably in second, though he wasn't anywhere near Nate. With Kyle in third and Ev in fourth, I knew my guy didn't have a chance at winning the challenge. But he still worked through the entire time, fighting as hard as he could to win.

And I respected that, deeply.

You could fake a lot of things in life, but passion? Drive? Those weren't among them.

Nate took his advantage and ran. No one was anywhere near close to him when he put the final piece in and stepped back to admire his work.

I sighed inwardly.

Kyle wasn't going on the last reward, which would mean worrying about him.

Worrying a lot.

I'd just have to survive it.

He caught my eye and winked at me while the other guys congratulated Nate, then he slapped Nate on the back before he stepped away.

At Jordan's instruction, I followed the men to the boat that would take me to the yacht. Though I wanted badly to look backward, I didn't let myself turn around.

I definitely couldn't put the target on Kyle at the last minute.

THE RIDE WAS SHORT, and we were seated at a table with a gorgeous view of the ocean soon enough. The yacht was moving smoothly, and I knew someone would be up with food for us anytime.

"So, who did Kyle pair you with? Reid or Ev?" Nate asked, curiosity in his voice. "I thought it was Ian for sure, up until he got voted out."

I frowned, my forehead creasing. There was no reason to keep up the charade, because Nate was automatically included in the final three and would have no say over the final vote. "What?"

"Kyle always works with the women to pair them off with whichever guy they choose. You're working with him, right?"

"I *am* working with him," I said. "But I didn't choose Reid or Ev. I picked Kyle."

Nate's eyes widened. "What?"

My lips curved upward.

"Fuck, he's good." The man leaned back in his chair, shaking his head. "Didn't see that coming. He looked like he'd given up before the season started."

"I think he had, but I wanted him before I ever made it to the island. He's a good guy."

"A damn good one," Nate admitted. "Did you know that all the men he paired off so far were the oldest ones?"

My eyebrows lifted. "Seriously?"

"Yep. No one's faded since Survival started. The closest guy to dying now is Colt, and he has a handful of years before he's gone. The only one close to going is Kyle."

"Damn. This game won't be the same without him," I said, though there was no sadness in my voice. As much as I liked watching him play, I liked watching him *live* a hell of a lot more.

"It won't, but I'll try to do what he's been doing. He just thinks I'm too nice for it."

I lifted an eyebrow. "Kyle told you you're too nice for matchmaking?"

"Too nice for *Survival*, actually."

I snorted. "Typical. Is he right?"

"Maybe." Nate shrugged, giving me a good-natured smile. "But I could do worse."

He had a point.

He'd made it to the final three, after all.

"Do you think Ev and Reid will work together to get rid of Kyle?" I asked, my nerves setting in again.

"Nah. Ev doesn't even want to be here. He's refused to strategize since your shitty date with him. Reid will vote with Kyle without a second thought."

I bit my lip. "I feel kind of bad for that date. And all the others."

"Don't. It's admirable not to lead anyone on. Losing would hurt a hell of a lot worse if we thought you might actually want us."

"I hope the other guys feel that way too."

"They do. And if they don't right now, they will when they've had time to think about it."

Our food arrived, and the conversation faded as we dug in.

If my final reward challenge couldn't be with Kyle, I was really, really glad it was Nate.

Even if I was struggling to contain my fear for the guy I was going to choose as my mate.

LAUNA

I WAS LEGITIMATELY SHAKING when the boat finally brought us back to the *Survival* island for the last time. My body trembled with the weight of my fear, no matter how hard I fought it.

Nate offered his arm to steady me, but I shook my head, shoving my hands in the stretchy pockets on my bike shorts. I didn't want to watch them quiver all the way to the last council.

We hiked all the way there in silence. The last guys were already waiting, having just recently finished their final vote.

I pled with the universe to let it be Kyle as we walked, repeating the words over and over again.

Please let him be here.

Please let him be here.

Please let him be here.

When we finally walked up the three stairs leading to the platform, and stepped into view of the remaining contestants, my entire body relaxed.

He was there.

Our eyes met immediately, and he grinned at me.

I didn't have it in me to smile back, but I finally started breathing normally again.

We'd made it.

We'd done it.

We survived.

Now, all there was left was to live our lives together.

The final moments of the game passed by in a blur.

Reid and Nate said a few words. Kyle told me he loved me again, much to Reid's shock.

I chose him, and he lifted my hand up, whooping the way he always did when he won a challenge.

I laughed.

We kissed.

And finally, it was over.

Kyle scooped me up and carried me away from the council area, his bare feet on the sand as he headed toward the private plane that waited for us.

The showrunner stepped into pace with him and offered us a few weeks at a vacation home, but Kyle's sister, Kenna, was getting married in a week and a half.

So, we'd take our vacation later.

There was life to live first.

ALL OF THE fae contestants would be traveling back home together, so they all piled into the plane after us. Kyle and I would need to have a lot of sex while I was adjusting to the change after sealing the bond, so we couldn't make things official until after the ride back home.

We snuggled in a chair together through the flight to Kyle's place. No one seemed angry with us, but they tried to give us privacy, and didn't really start conversations with us.

We were quiet through most of the flight.

The fact that we'd survived and won the game together was still setting in, and it felt insanely surreal.

He hadn't been home in six months, so I wasn't sure how he was feeling about that. It seemed like too private of a question in a plane full of other people, so I didn't ask.

As weird as the situation was for me, I knew it had to be weirder after six entire months playing a game with the men around us. He'd only had a few days off between each season. That had to do a number to a person's—or fae's—mind.

Both of us dozed on and off through the long flight back, and when the plane finally landed, I saw the relief in everyone's eyes.

We were all done.

The guys all said their goodbyes after we got off the plane. Some of them traded bro-hugs, and I noticed that everyone except Travis hugged Kyle.

A few of them nodded at me, grinned at me, or congratulated me for the way I'd played them. I smiled and thanked them, still blushing but no longer actively avoiding them.

When the goodbyes were over, Kyle put an arm over my shoulders and pulled me to his side. We walked together to the armored vehicle the Society had provided, and slipped into the back one after another.

I watched the scenery all the way to his house, leaning against his side as we drove. There was a divider between us and the driver, so we couldn't see them, and they couldn't see us.

Kyle's hand cupped one of my breasts partway through the drive.

The touch was nice, and made me itch even more to get out of my sandy *Survival* clothing. It would've felt much better if I was naked.

He slowly dragged his thumb over my nipple, and I bit my lip as we flew down the beachside highway.

Desire pooled between my thighs as he continued touching me.

Teasing me.

Making me want him.

I set my hand over his erection when I was too horny to think straight, and his chest rumbled lightly for me.

I gripped him through his shorts, and he kissed the side of my neck, sucking lightly.

"When we get home, I want you sprawled out on my kitchen counter, naked," he murmured, low enough that the driver wouldn't hear.

"What are you going to do to me?" I stroked his cock lightly, over his shorts.

"First, I'm going to take you hard and fast. Make you mine. When the bond's started and you've gotten your wings, I'll take my time with you. Open your legs up and lick our pleasure off your pretty little cunt. Watch you come on my fingers. Taste you on my tongue some more."

My chest rose and fell rapidly.

"When you feel so good you can't think straight, I'll roll you onto your stomach and take you from behind."

"Fast and hard again?"

"No, Beautiful. I want you slow, so I know you can feel every fucking inch of me rubbing over every gorgeous part of your channel. When we finally leave the kitchen, you'll know I've claimed you so completely that I'm never letting go."

I could've climaxed there and then, if he touched my clit just a little.

But, he didn't.

He just kept playing with my breasts and sucking on my neck until the driver finally made it through the gates and parked in front of his house.

Everything was a blur as Kyle thanked the driver and walked me up to the double doors, the back of my body pressed to the front of his. I was so wet between my thighs, I felt my desire drip down the inside of my leg.

He typed a code into a keypad, unlocking it.

We didn't make it to the kitchen, though.

As soon as they were closed behind us, Kyle had me pinned to one of the doors, his mouth taking mine in a deliciously brutal kiss. It didn't feel like kissing—it felt like making love.

"I need you now," he growled against my swollen lips, when he finally pulled back for air. He was already pushing my shorts and swim bottoms down, knowing I wanted him as much as he wanted me.

Kyle recaptured my mouth, and kissed me as I stepped out of my shorts and bottoms.

As he shoved his own to the ground.

As he ripped my t-shirt down the middle, and tore the bikini top I never wanted to see again.

One of his hands squeezed my breast.

The other grabbed my ass.

I hooked a leg around his hip and lined him up with my entrance, done waiting for him. He'd said *now*, and I'd been ready before we were both naked.

When I arched to take him inside me, he moved with me.

I gasped at the sudden feeling of his entire cock filling me.

"You feel so good," I breathed.

"I've got nothing on you." He pushed in a little deeper, and I moaned.

"I'm not going to last."

"You're not finishing until you're mine, Beautiful."

He grabbed my other leg, hauling me higher and changing the angle. I sucked in a breath at the sudden change in position.

"I'm yours, Kyle," I whispered.

The words still felt like magic.

"Louder." His command was strained. His wings unfurled behind him, his horns spiraling off his head.

"I'm yours!" I yelled, my voice echoing through the massive house I hadn't even seen yet.

"And I'm yours, for the rest of our eternity." His words came out a growl, and lightning raced down my spine.

I screamed at the sudden burst of pain and pleasure, the most intense orgasm of my life taking hold of me.

My body rocked and arched and moved.

A new weight settled on my back—it had to be my wings.

My pleasure was so all-consuming that I barely felt them.

My eyes were locked with Kyle's as we came down from our high together. Though the magic between us was fading slightly, there was no denying that something had changed.

We were connected, now.

Permanently.

"I really hope you don't regret this," I whispered, unable to help myself.

Fire blazed to life in his eyes. "You saved my life, Beautiful. I don't regret a damn thing, and I never will. Do you regret it?"

"Of course not."

"Then don't suggest that I do. We're mates, Launa. For better or worse, for the rest of our lives and long after we're gone." He kissed me again, slowly.

Softly.
Sweetly.

It made my chest ache, and felt like something straight out of a romance book.

"Okay," I said.

"Now, I want to keep this going..." he adjusted his grip on my ass and thighs. "But we need showers and food. What do you think about making a stop in the kitchen, then heading straight for the tub?"

After the glorious bath we'd shared at the spa, I'd never say no to bathing with him. We'd rinsed off in the shower first, so I assumed we'd do the same.

"Sounds amazing."

"Good." He kissed me again, then carried me into the kitchen, his cock still buried inside me. "You look damn good with wings, for the record."

I'd forgotten about the wings.

"Can I take a bath with them?" I asked.

"Assuming you straddle me."

The wickedness in his eyes made me certain that had been his plan from the beginning.

I smiled. "I can probably handle that."

He grinned, and gave me one last kiss before he opened up the fridge.

The kitchen was modern, with gorgeous black cabinets and gray countertops. The walls were a crisp white that made everything look brighter. Though the decorations were sparse, they were mostly small plants that softened up the room's sharpness.

Five minutes later, he held me to his chest with one arm and held a massive casserole dish of gluten-free pasta someone had premade for us in the other.

I looked around curiously as he carried both me and the food through the house

The staircase we passed was made of the same sleek flooring as the kitchen and entryway. The style of the walls and everything else carried through the massive office we passed, as well as the huge gym.

It was the same in Kyle's bedroom—our bedroom—but cozier. The crisp white had been traded for a soft, light gray. The statement wall was a charcoal shade that complimented it. Much of the cold floor was covered with a thick, luxurious rug.

"It's gorgeous," I admitted, as he carried me right into the bathroom.

I swear, any blogger would've been jealous of it.

There was a massive, marble free-standing tub.

The walk-in shower was big enough for three or four people, with just as many showerheads.

Kyle didn't waste any time as he set me down on the countertop and put the pasta next to me. Worried it would scald the gorgeous countertops, I quickly lifted it onto my lap, wincing at the heat.

Yeah, that was hot.

I'd be fine, though.

Kyle turned the water on before realizing what I was doing. "What the hell, Beautiful?" he plucked the dish off my legs, dropping it on the counter before smoothing his hands over the hot skin on my thighs.

"I don't want to burn the counter," I explained.

"I don't give a fuck about that. These legs, though?" He bent over and brushed his lips against the front of one, then dragged his tongue over my skin. "These, I care about. Don't risk yourself."

"It wasn't *risky*."

"Maybe not, but I don't want you hurting." He grabbed a fork, and handed one to me. "Here, let's eat while the tub fills. We'll rinse off when we're done."

I agreed, and we dug in together.

After we were full, we showered quickly, and climbed into the tub together.

LAUNA

AT LEAST TWO hours had gone by when we finally made it out of the tub.

Some sex had occurred.

Plenty of sex.

We were drying off when the doorbell rang.

I frowned, looking at Kyle.

He grinned sheepishly. "Probably my family. I'm sure they think I lost."

"You don't think anyone told them?"

"Nah. We don't have connections like some of the other guys. They'll be shocked when they meet you."

I bit my lip.

The doorbell rang again.

And again.

"We'd better get dressed quick. They have the code," he said, towing me toward the closet.

"Um, *why* do they have the code?" I demanded.

He flashed me a grin. "Don't worry, Beautiful. They can't usually get in and out whenever they want. I just wanted them to check on my house now and then while I was on the island."

Okay, that made sense.

"We're going to change it, right?"

"As soon as I find my phone and power it up enough to send a text to my security company."

That was fair.

Reasonable, even.

Sure enough, I heard the front door open a moment later. We hadn't bothered closing our bedroom door, so it was way too accessible.

Kyle tugged a pair of sweats up his legs, and I couldn't help but admire his ass.

Damn, it was the perfect bubble shape.

"Stare at me *after* you're dressed," he said, putting a gigantic, black long-sleeved shirt in my hands.

"Alright." I slipped the shirt over my head. He did the same, though his was a thin white t-shirt. And the clothes actually fit him.

"Kyle?" A woman's voice demanded.

"It's Kenna," he murmured. "I'm sure my parents are with her.

"I brought ice cream and board games! No one is moping!" She said, her voice ringing through the house.

The woman was certainly commanding. I had to respect her for it, though it seemed safe to assume it would irritate me from time to time.

"Just a second," Kyle called out. "Getting dressed."

"He doesn't sound like he's moping," another woman said.

"Thank fuck," Kenna replied.

"Language," a male voice grumbled.

"Are you sure you want me to meet them right now, looking like this?" I whispered to Kyle, as I stepped into the pair of boxer briefs he'd handed me. I didn't love that they fit just fine, but I wasn't going to think about that for too long.

"Wearing my clothes, looking like you just spent two hours fucking me in the bathtub?" he asked, lifting his eyebrows as his lips stretched in another grin. "I can't think of a better way."

He kissed me, then towed me out of the closet behind him. Part of me wanted to dig in my heels and refuse to go any further, but I knew that was ridiculous. There was no point in putting off the meeting, despite my attempt at convincing him otherwise.

As soon as he stepped through the doorway, someone threw their arms around him.

I stopped abruptly, barely managing not to run into his back. And the person's arms.

Another set of arms joined.

Kyle hugged both of his assailants with his free arm, though he maintained his grip on my hand. It steadied me, honestly, so I was grateful that he did.

"We'll make the last few months fun," his mother whispered.

"You won't miss anything," Kenna added, her voice growing a little tighter.

They finally released him, both of them stepping back.

"Thanks for the offer," Kyle said. "But I've got other plans."

A moment of silence passed.

And another.

"What the hell does that mean?" Kenna finally asked.

I could hear the grin in Kyle's voice when he said, "I've got someone to introduce you to."

Someone sucked in a breath.

Kenna breathed, "*No*."

He stepped back, pulling me in front of him and setting his hands on my waist but leaving space between his chest and my wings. I appreciated that, *tremendously*. They were insanely sensitive.

"This is Launa. My mate."

His mom gasped. She looked about the same age as us, considering she was fae, but her hair was the same shade as his. Their eyes were the same shape, and their bone structure was insanely similar, too. He clearly took after her.

"You did it," Kenna said, her eyes wide and her lips round. "I can't believe it."

"*We* did it," he said, and I could hear that smile again.

"*You* did it," I admitted, looking back at him over my shoulder.

His smile widened. "A little."

Kyle's mom surged forward, flinging her arms around me and squeezing tightly. I bit my lip to stop from crying out at the bump to my wings, and hugged her back. She obviously wasn't *trying* to hurt me.

"Easy, now. Her wings are sensitive," Kyle said, his hands tightening protectively on my waist.

"You're not dying," Kenna said.

"Nope." He popped his lips with the 'p' as his mom released me. Her eyes were brimmed with tears as she whispered,

"*Thank you.*"

"I'm lucky to have him," I said, giving her a small but genuine smile.

"Like hell you are. This bastard does *not* deserve you," Kenna warned, stepping up next to her mom and hugging me too. Her hug was gentler, surprisingly.

I laughed, and Kyle did too. "She's stuck with me anyway," he said, squeezing my hip lightly.

Kenna released me, and Kyle's dad stepped forward with a grin and an offer of his hand.

"Welcome to the family, Launa."

His words nearly made my eyes sting. "Thank you."

"Now, let's play those board games," Kenna said, gesturing toward the kitchen. "I already told Todd to find something else to do for a few hours, so I'm free."

"Kenna," their mom said, rolling her eyes as she looped her arm through her daughter's. "They need space for the next few days. You can avoid your wedding stress through board games after they've adjusted."

I shot her a grateful look.

Kyle made a noise of agreement. "Sorry, Squirt. Door's closed for about a week."

She huffed, but agreed.

Kyle's dad smacked him on the shoulder lightly, offering him a congrats as the three of them headed out.

When the door was shut behind them, I breathed a little easier.

"Well, that could've been worse," Kyle said cheerfully.

I couldn't help but laugh.

He was right; it could've been *much* worse.

Maybe I really would like his family.

He turned me around and kissed me gently. "Now, I'm going to find my phone so I can reset that code. Do you want to get a movie playing in our room, and spend the rest of the day in bed together?"

"That sounds perfect," I admitted.

His smile widened, and he kissed me again. "Good."

With that, he grabbed my ass, making me laugh again before he disappeared.

I padded back into *our* bedroom with a smile on my face.

Fighting to play on *Survival* was so, so worth it.

twelve

KYLE

THE NEXT FEW weeks passed quickly.

By some miracle, my family actually gave us privacy for about a week and a half. After that, Kenna was strung-up so tightly with nerves that they got a little needy.

Thankfully, the need was appeased through strategic board games.

Launa won more often than she didn't, which made me proud. She would've slain those puzzle challenges that kicked my ass.

The rest of us pulled out a win about a third of the time, combined, but none of us minded.

And we were figuring out which kinds of games she *wasn't* killer at, which made her laugh.

She was laid-back enough that her and Kenna didn't butt heads. When Kenna got a little bitchy, Launa had no problem standing up to her. The two became surprisingly fast friends.

The wedding arrived quickly, and more friends were made leading up to it. Launa hit it off with the five Survival girls who had played before her—Molly, Erin, Ann, Lisa, and Eve—and they all gushed about how much they loved the way she played.

Plans were put on the calendar for them to hang out after the festivities were over.

I didn't miss the gleam of emotion in my woman's eyes when she thanked me for befriending the girls first, making it easier for her.

I just rolled my eyes at her, reminding her that she was the one they wanted to hang out with.

When the remark earned me a bright, emotional smile, I kissed her.

Then made love to her.

Being mated was absolute bliss.

I shed a tear or two when I watched my sister say "I do" with the guy Rhett had found for her, and clapped him on the back in thanks when I bumped into him during the reception.

Then, I dragged my mate out onto the dance floor and spent all night with her in my arms. The bulge of a ring box in my pocket had been pushing me to make my move all day, but I wasn't about to interrupt my sister's wedding. After the wedding was over, I'd get Launa alone.

When the DJ played the last slow song of the night, the bride and groom already gone to seal their bond, I lowered my lips to Launa's ear. She tipped her head a little, making it easier to hear me.

"What would you say if I asked you to marry me, Beautiful?"

Her lips curved upward, and it was my turn to give her my ear. "We're already mated, Kyle."

I chuckled, making my way off the dance floor with her. She shot me a curious look when I led her out of the room, away from all the people there, and onto a balcony I'd made sure was lined with lights and flowers.

When I got down on one knee in front of her, her eyes widened, and flooded with tears.

"What do you say, Beautiful? Will you throw a party with me, and agree to be mine the human way too?"

She jerked her head in a nod, "Yes. Definitely."

Before I could get up, she grabbed my face and kissed me, hard.

Passionately.

The way I wanted to fuck her.

That would have to wait until we got home, though.

I was hard and she was *breathing* hard, when she finally pulled away. "Can I see the ring?"

"Of course." I slipped it onto her finger, and she bit her lip as she stared down at it.

"You're too good to me."

I grinned, and kissed her again. "Not possible."

She buried her fingers in my hair and let me pin her to the wall for a solid ten minutes before someone yelled at us from the manicured garden below. When we separated, her cheeks were flushed with that sexy blush, and we were both breathing hard.

She smiled at me, and I grinned back.

Playing Survival was the best decision I'd ever made.

I was the luckiest bastard in the world.

epilogue

LAUNA—A FEW MONTHS LATER

"IT'S TIME," Molly said, her expression serious. "Do you have the EpiPen?" She looked at Erin.

"Right here." Erin lifted it off the countertop, swinging it lazily.

"Not a fucking chance." Kyle plucked it from my redheaded friend.

As much as I liked the other Survival girls, I'd gotten much closer to Molly and Erin than them. It helped that Kyle had become really good friends with Cameron and Rhett, too, so we all had fun.

And considering that all three of us couples had been elected to lead the Society together shortly after Kenna's wedding?

Even more closeness had ensued.

The Society as a whole had been so inspired watching Kyle fight for the other men that he'd become an automatic choice for the third leading seat. I was just there because I was with him.

But, I did work well with the other girls.

And though I'd always love my research, I *was* passionate about the game shows. Constantly brain-storming new things for them was a ton of fun.

"You want us to believe *you're* going to stab her with that thing?" Erin asked, her voice skeptical as she gestured to the EpiPen Kyle had snagged.

"If the alternative is watching her airway close up after she eats real pasta, you can be damn sure I'll stab her." He looked at me. "Carefully."

"I believe you," I promised.

"She's not going to have a reaction to this. Fae *don't* have allergies," Cameron said. He'd been saying as much for months, but all of us ignored him. He was technically the Society's leader, alongside Molly, but that didn't make him our boss.

"Just eat the damn spaghetti already," Rhett huffed, gesturing to the bowl in Molly's hands.

"You don't have to do this," she reminded me, flat-out ignoring her mate and Erin's for the moment.

"I want to," I said, accepting the bowl when she handed it to me.

"Should we chant?" Erin checked.

"Of course we should chant," Kyle said, making a fist with the hand that didn't hold the EpiPen. "Laun-a. Laun-a. Laun-a."

Everyone joined in.

My face was burning, but I couldn't stop myself from grinning.

And even though it was absolutely ridiculous, I wrapped my fork in *real* pasta and lifted the bite to my mouth.

Cheers and whoops erupted as I took a bite, groaning.

It was *so much* better than the gluten-free stuff.

"Well?" Erin demanded.

"Give her a few minutes," Molly warned.

I chewed and swallowed.

Cameron turned on music while we waited.

Kyle plopped down on the kitchen bench beside me, the Epi-Pen at the ready.

After a few minutes, I let out a pent-up breath. "My throat's not closing. My stomach's not turning. I think we're good."

Everyone cheered again, and Cam declared, "Let's bring out the ice cream!"

My mouth watered, and I couldn't wipe the grin off my face.

I was *made* to be a fae.

afterthoughts

Okay, I love novellas.

They're so intensely satisfying to write, because of how fast things go.

I LOVE the representation of real *Survivor* that this is. Because some seasons are wild and chaotic, and others are not. Considering Kyle's friendships and reputation, it just made sense for his story to be a simple one. Adding Launa to the picture seemed natural.

I'm sure some of you are disappointed that Kyle's book turned into a novella, and that's totally fair. But ultimately, I didn't have enough inspiration to make it any longer. My options were to drag it out torturously, not write it at all, or let it be short, and I went with the last one.

And truthfully? I love short books. I know there are always people who want longer books, but is there anyone other than me who loves a good, satisfying bite-sized read? Give me a solid romance I can read in the bathtub in an hour or two, and I'm a happy woman.

I hope you loved Kyle's story!
Until next time!
All the love,
Lola Glass <3

stay in touch

If you want to receive Lola's newsletter for new releases (no spam!) use this link:

LINK

Or find her on:
FACEBOOK
TIKTOK
INSTAGRAM
PINTEREST
GOODREADS

More of the Mac...

all series by lola glass

Standalones:

Survival of the Mated

Mate Mountain

Wildwood

Deceit & Devotion

Claimed by the Wolf

Forbidden Mates

Wild Hunt

Kings of Disaster

Night's Curse

Outcast Pack

Feral Pack

Mate Hunt

Series:

Burning Kingdom

Sacrificed to the Fae King

Shifter Queen

Wolfsbane

Shifter City

Supernatural Underworld

Moon of the Monsters

Rejected Mate Refuge

about the author

Lola is a book-lover with a *slight* romance obsession and a passion for love—real love. Not the flowers-and-chocolates kind of love, but the kind where two people build a relationship strong enough to last. That's the kind of relationship she loves to read about, and the kind she tries to portray in her books.

Even though they're fun stories about sassy women and huge, growly magical men ;)

www.ingramcontent.com/pod-product-compliance
Lightning Source LLC
Chambersburg PA
CBHW010424120726
47992CB00008B/3320